PUFFIN BOOKS

MRS PEPPERPOT'S YEAR

It was New Year's Eve, and Mrs Pepperpot was just putting the cat out when suddenly – she SHRANK!

If you have met Mrs Pepperpot before, you will know that she had the unfortunate habit of turning small – just the size of a pepperpot – at the most inconvenient moments.

'Good gracious!' cried Mrs Pepperpot this time, as she rolled over in the snow.

'What a bit of luck!' said the cat (for Mrs Pepperpot could understand animal language when she went small). 'Now you can come along and see something no human has ever seen.'

Then Mrs Pepperpot, who wasn't a bit scared, jumped on the cat's back and went to see what she could see. Something interesting always happened when she shrank. This time she helped the animals turn over the big brown bear so that his temper wouldn't be too unbearable (!) when he woke in the spring, but on another occasion she fell in a mother hen's nest and got bossed around with all the chicks, and once she went small when she was in hospital, and a little girl called Rose had to put her to bed in a chocolate box with a hankie as a sheet. Yes, it was always very interesting, but when it was all over Mrs Pepperpot was usually more than thankful to return safely home again, to her right size and her husband, Mr Pepperpot.

Alf Prøysen was born in Norway in 1914. He started writing when he was twenty and wrote many successful children's books. He also produced a programme for children on radio and wrote a weekly column in a leading Norwegian newspaper. He died in 1971.

Mrs Pepperpot's Year

Stories by
ALF PRØYSEN

TRANSLATED BY MARIANNE HELWEG

ILLUSTRATIONS BY BJÖRN BERG

PUFFIN BOOKS

PUFFIN BOOKS

Penguin Books Ltd, 27 Wrights Lane, London W8 5TZ (Publishing and Editorial)
and Harmondsworth, Middlesex, England (Distribution and Warehouse)
Viking Penguin Inc., 40 West 23rd Street, New York, New York 10010, USA
Penguin Books Australia Ltd, Ringwood, Victoria, Australia
Penguin Books Canada Ltd, 2801 John Street, Markham, Ontario, Canada L3R 1B4
Penguin Books (NZ) Ltd, 182–190 Wairau Road, Auckland 10, New Zealand

This selection first published by Hutchinson Junior Books Ltd 1973
Published in Puffin Books 1980
Reprinted 1981, 1982 (twice), 1983, 1984, 1985, 1986, 1987

This selection copyright © Hutchinson Junior Books Ltd, 1973
English translation copyright © Hutchinson Junior Books Ltd, 1973
Illustrations to stories 6, 7, 8, 10 and 12 copyright © Hutchinson
Junior Books Ltd, 1973
All rights reserved

Set, printed and bound in Great Britain by
Cox & Wyman Ltd, Reading
Set in Monotype Baskerville

Contents

The New Year's Eve adventure

IT HAPPENED every New Year's Eve. Mrs Pepperpot would say to herself: 'This year I really will watch the fireworks and listen to the church bells ringing in the New Year.'

Mr Pepperpot said the same. They would dress up in their best clothes, and sit down to a meal of boiled bacon and dumplings, followed by Mrs Pepperpot's special little cakes with cloudberry jam and whipped cream. Afterwards they would each sit in their favourite chair and read the magazines they had got for Christmas.

The only sound was the ticking of the clock; tick, tock, tick, tock . . .

After a while Mrs Pepperpot would begin to feel sleepy, so she got up and made some coffee. When they had drunk the coffee, Mr Pepperpot would walk to the window to see if there were any rockets going off.

7

So the hours went by and when the clock finally struck twelve and the rockets shot up in great arches through the sky and the bell-ringer started pulling the rope in the bell-tower, well . . . you've guessed it . . . Mr and Mrs Pepperpot would be fast asleep in their chairs and never hear a thing.

So this year they decided not to bother to stay up, but just go to bed at their usual hour. When they had eaten their supper and drunk their coffee they sat reading their magazines till they got sleepy. First Mr Pepperpot started stretching and yawning.

'I think I'll turn in,' he muttered.

'You do that,' said Mrs Pepperpot, who had been looking at the same page of her magazine for the last twenty minutes. 'I'll just let the cat out. Come on, Pussy,' she called, 'you're going out in the snow.'

She followed the cat on to the doorstep and looked up at the moon to see if there was a ring round it.

Just at that moment she SHRANK!

If you've met Mrs Pepperpot before, you will

know that she has this unfortunate habit of turning small – just the size of a pepperpot – at the most inconvenient times.

'Goodness gracious!' she cried as she rolled over in the snow.

'What a bit of luck!' said the cat. 'Now you can come along with me and see something no human has ever seen. Jump on my back!'

That's another thing that happens when Mrs Pepperpot turns small; she can understand animal language and they can understand her.

'Well, if it's really special . . .' said Mrs Pepperpot, climbing on to Pussy's back, 'but I must be back home when they ring the New Year in.'

The cat set off with Mrs Pepperpot on her back. It was very dark and the wind was blowing snow in her face, but she could tell they were going up the side of the mountain. Through the trees she could hear the sound of heavy feet and crashing branches, and as the moon came out from behind the clouds, she could see it was a big bull moose with his family behind him. In the tree-tops she could hear the squirrel chattering and above her head came the whirring sound of grouse wings. There was an owl hooting and a fox barking, and she could see the darting shapes of hares as they zigzagged across the snow or ran round in a ring. But they were all going the same way and at last they stopped in front of a huge rock-face.

'What are they all stopping for?' whispered Mrs Pepperpot, putting her mouth very close to the cat's ear.

'They're listening; don't you hear it yourself?' answered the cat.

Mrs Pepperpot listened and after a moment she *did* hear something; it sounded like the faint rumble of a motor-bike, very far away.

'That's him all right, snoring!' said the cat.

'Will you please explain?' Mrs Pepperpot said. She was getting tired of all this mystery.

'Well,' said the cat, 'behind that rock is the winter lair of the king of the forest, the big brown bear. He's been sleeping in there for several months now, but on New Year's Eve he has to turn over on his other side.'

'What happens if he doesn't turn over?' asked Mrs Pepperpot.

'Oh, it's terrible!' said the cat, 'if he lies on the same side all the winter, you see, he wakes up in the spring in a very bad mood, all stiff and sore. Then he takes it out on the rest of us and woe-betide any animal that gets in his way!'

'Well,' said Mrs Pepperpot, 'how d'you get him to turn over?'

'We make all the noise we can, but it's getting more and more difficult each year, as the King is getting older and deafer. We had a real job rousing him last year,' said the cat.

None of the other animals had said anything up to now, they were all so busy getting their breath back. But now one of the hares, gleaming in his white winter coat, spoke up:

'What we need is a new sort of noise – much sharper than all this yowling of foxes, and tooting of owls – a bit of dynamite would be good, like the men use when they're blasting holes in the rocks.'

Mrs Pepperpot snapped her fingers: 'That gives me an idea! I have just what we need at

11

home. But I shall need some help,' Mrs Pepperpot was thinking hard as she spoke.

The bull moose was standing close by. He
looked as big as a house from down there, but
she cupped her hands and shouted up to him:

'Hi, Moose! Can you carry me back to my
house? I want to fetch my box of tricks.'

The moose at once knelt down in the snow, so
that Mrs Pepperpot could climb on to his head,
where she settled herself between his antlers.

'Right, let's go!' she shouted.

In no time at all the moose had run down the
mountain to the valley and then up the hill to
Mrs Pepperpot's house.

'You'll have to be very quiet,' said Mrs Pepperpot as the moose knelt down to let her slide off his neck. 'We don't want to scare my husband.'

Luckily the door to the outhouse was open,

and there were no dogs or cats or hens in there to raise the alarm. Mrs Pepperpot went straight over to a large carton covered in paper and carefully tied with string.

'In this box there are enough bangs to wake a cartload of bears,' she told the moose, who was standing quietly in the doorway.

Over the years Mrs Pepperpot had bought firecrackers and rockets and roman candles and so on to let off on New Year's Eve, but as they were never used, she had quite a big collection.

Now the problem was how to get the box hitched on to the moose, so that he could drag it back up the mountain to the bear's lair. Mrs Pepperpot got him to kneel down again, then she fastened a rope first round the carton and then round the moose's antlers. Then she swung herself back into her 'saddle' on his knobbly forehead, and away they went down the hill, the carton lurching along like a crazy toboggan.

'I hope the fireworks don't blow up on the way,' thought Mrs Pepperpot, but she said nothing to the moose, who was carefully avoiding the trees as they climbed up the mountain.

Luckily the snow was thick enough to make a smooth path for the box, which was not very heavy.

The birds and the animals were all waiting for them when they arrived.

'Come on, everybody!' shouted Mrs Pepperpot as she jumped down into the snow, 'help me get the string and the paper off.'

The owl and the grouse pecked away at the string, and the foxes used their sharp claws to tear off the paper. At last Mrs Pepperpot could open the box.

'There you are, children,' she said, 'every kind of banger and firecracker you can think of. If His Majesty King Bear doesn't wake up when this lot goes off, you can take it from me he's dead!'

'How will you light them?' asked the white-coated hare who had suggested dynamite.

'Good question!' said Mrs Pepperpot, 'but luckily I had a box of matches in my apron pocket when I turned small.'

But first she told all the birds and animals to stand well out of the way. All except her faithful friend, the squirrel, who had helped her many times before. Sitting on his back, she told him to climb a few feet up a tall pine tree near the box. From there she struck all the matches at once and threw them into the box.

'Now shin up to the top as fast as you can,' she shouted, as the first bangers started going off. The squirrel kept to the far side of the tree-trunk, and when he got to the top he took a flying leap to the next tree, where they landed safely and well out of reach of any flying missiles.

'Phew! That was a near thing!' gasped Mrs Pepperpot, who had been more frightened by the squirrel's aerobatics than the hissing and popping that was going on below.

Looking down from so high, it really was a spectacular show, as the whole box of fireworks went up in one colossal din and blaze. It lit up the snow, the trees, the sky and the animals and birds scattering in every direction.

As the last bangers fizzled out and the sky grew dark again, Mrs Pepperpot heard a very different sound, and so did all the animals and

birds; it was like the creaking of a heavy door followed by a long, loud 'Yaaaaaawn!'

'Hooray!' shouted all the animals and the birds squawked excitedly; 'King Bear has turned! King Bear has turned!'

The squirrel carried Mrs Pepperpot down to the ground and she found herself surrounded by stamping feet and flapping wings; everyone wanted to thank her.

'Help, help!' she cried, 'you're smothering me!'

But the next moment she was back to her normal size, standing in the snow by the big rock-face.

Every bird, every animal had vanished in the darkness – except one. Mrs Pepperpot felt warm fur rubbing against her leg.

'Is that you, Pussy?' she said, picking up the purring cat. 'Well, you certainly gave me a New Year adventure this year!'

And as she trudged back home through the snow, the church bells began to ring out and beautiful rockets lit up the sky over the village.

Fate and Mrs Pepperpot

MRS PEPPERPOT is fond of fortune-telling, but she only does it for herself, never for other people. When she has finished a cup of coffee, she likes to peer at the grounds at the bottom of the cup to see what fortune has in store for her.

This was what she was doing one cold morning in January. 'My goodness!' she exclaimed excitedly. 'I can see a long journey over water! I knew my luck would change. Now all I have to do is pack my bag and wait for it to happen.'

She was just about to go up to the attic for her old suitcase, when she remembered that she had dipped her biscuit in the coffee, so there were biscuit crumbs mixed with the grounds and that didn't count.

'Ah well,' she sighed, 'I suppose I couldn't really expect it. And what would Mr Pepperpot

do if I went off by myself on a holiday in the middle of winter?'

She picked up the magazine that was lying on the table. It was open at the page headed 'The Stars and You'. She looked under Taurus, for her birthday was in May. It said: 'Prepare for a journey over water.'

This was astonishing!

'It *must* be fate!' said Mrs Pepperpot. 'This time there's no denying it. I will pack at once.'

Then she glanced at the date of the magazine; it was a year old!

'I might have known it,' she said disgustedly, as she threw the paper into the stove. 'Anyway, who wants to go trapesing off to the south of France or wherever. I'm all right here, aren't I? Got my husband and my house to look after and my cat . . .' She got up and started bustling about, sweeping the floor, cleaning out the sink and peeling the potatoes for supper. But just as she was standing there, she suddenly felt a tingling in the sole of her right foot. She waited for a moment; yes, it was quite definitely tingling!

'That settles it,' she said firmly to herself, as she went up to the attic to fetch her suitcase.

Tingling under your right foot, you see, is another sign that you are going on a journey, and this time Mrs Pepperpot was quite sure there was no mistake.

She came down with the battered old suitcase. 'Long time since you've had an airing,' she said, looking at it ruefully. 'Never mind. Next thing is to wash all my clothes to be ready for the trip.'

But she found she had no wash-powder, so she put on her hat and coat and a warm muffler and set out for the shop.

The shop was full of customers. At the door stood a lady with a handful of brochures. She was advertising a new wash-powder.

'This product is not like any you have used before,' she was saying, 'it will take all the work out of washing-day.'

'Can't fool me with that sort of nonsense,' muttered Mrs Pepperpot. But the lady went on: 'In every packet you buy today there is a numbered coupon, and one of those has a lucky number. Whoever gets the lucky number will win a seven-day sunshine holiday for two at beautiful Las Palmas in the Canary Islands. Don't miss this chance, ladies and gentlemen, the lucky number will be drawn tonight and displayed in the shop-window at closing time.'

She hadn't finished speaking before everyone started grabbing the packets of wash-powder. Some bought as many as six!

'Take them all year to get through that lot,'

muttered Mrs Pepperpot. She just bought one packet.

'That's all I need for *my* lucky number,' she said as she trudged home through the snow. She was just wondering whom she should invite to go with her on her sunshine holiday, Mrs North, perhaps, or Mrs West, when whoops! her feet slid from under her and she SHRANK!

She had been walking on the path where the snow was soft and not too slippery, but now both she and the packet tumbled on to the glass-hard surface of the road, just where it sloped steeply down towards the stream.

'Oh me, oh my!' she moaned, as she started to slide after the packet. 'This is a journey all right, but not quite what I intended.'

Faster and faster they went, till wham! The packet struck a tree-stump just by the edge of the stream. Mrs Pepperpot landed on top of the packet and the force of it pushed them both into the icy water!

Off they went again, whirling and bobbing in the fast-flowing stream, Mrs Pepperpot clinging on as best she could.

'Skipper of my own yacht on a luxury cruise!'
she joked, but she didn't feel very cheerful. 'Not
much hope of rescue here, I'm afraid.'

'Caw, caw!' croaked a voice from above.
'Don't say that!' And before she had time to see
who was there, she had been picked up by her
skirt and set down again on the bank of the
stream.

Mrs Pepperpot blinked at her rescuer, a big black crow.

'Thanks, pal, that wasn't a minute too soon! But could you please hurry after my packet and rescue that too?'

'Caw, caw! Right you are!' cried the crow, swooping and darting after the swirling packet till he could get a hold on it with his beak.

With some difficulty he hauled it to the bank where Mrs Pepperpot stood ready to help pull it out of the water.

'I'm afraid your wash-powder will be a bit soggy by now,' said the crow, when they had got it safely on land.

'Never mind,' said Mrs Pepperpot, 'thanks to you, I can still believe in my lucky day.'

'Anything to oblige, Mrs P. Many's the nice piece of bacon rind I've had at your back door. Glad to get a chance to do you a good turn.'

There the conversation came to an end, because Mrs Pepperpot grew to her normal size and the crow flew off. But she waved to him as she hurried home with her wet packet under her arm.

Indoors she emptied the packet into a bowl, carefully taking out the coupon which she put to dry on a towel. She noted the number: 347.

'That's good,' she said, 'it has a seven in it. Sure to be a winner.'

Then she set to with her washing and she worked so hard, she never noticed the time, till she heard Mr Pepperpot open the front door.

'Hallo, my love!' he shouted, 'you'll never guess my luck!'

Mrs Pepperpot stared at him; in one hand he held a packet of the same wash-powder she had bought, and in the other a coupon!

'Let me tell you!' went on Mr Pepperpot excitedly. 'I went to the shop this morning on my way to work to get some baccy, and there was this lady . . .'

'I know,' said Mrs Pepperpot, 'I saw her too.'

'You did? Well, of course I bought a packet of her wash-powder – come in handy, I thought, and you never know – stand as good a chance as anyone else . . .'

Mrs Pepperpot couldn't bear the suspense any longer: 'Come to the point, man!'

'All right, all right! I just went back to look at the number in the window and it's the same as mine! 693.'

Mrs Pepperpot turned her head away.

'Congratulations,' she said. 'I hope you have a very nice trip.'

'Well!' said her husband, 'you don't sound very enthusiastic. Don't you want to go on a sunshine holiday to the Canary Islands?'

'But . . . but . . .' stammered Mrs Pepperpot. 'How was I to know you'd be taking *me*?'

'You silly old thing – who else?' laughed Mr Pepperpot and gave her a smacking kiss.

Mrs Pepperpot helps Arne

Mr and Mrs Pepperpot *did* enjoy their holidays in the Canaries and Mrs Pepperpot never shrank the whole time they were there. They bathed in the sea and got brown lying in the sun and in the evenings they listened to the music in the restaurant and tried the strange food they were served.

But at the end of the seven days they were quite glad to go home to Norway with all its ice and snow. It was nice, too, to get back to their own little house on the hill, and to sit down to their favourite supper of fried herring and boiled potatoes, followed by pancakes and bilberry jam.

'They can keep their foreign la-di-da meals,' said Mr Pepperpot, 'my wife's cooking is good enough for me!'

'I'll remember that next time you grumble!' said Mrs Pepperpot.

So the wintry days went on and soon it was time for the school-children to have their half-term holiday. Most of them were keen skiers and this meant they could ski all day every day for a whole week!

Mrs Pepperpot could hear them shouting and laughing as they rushed down the slopes near her house.

But one day when she was baking bread in the kitchen, she looked out of the window and saw a little boy making his way slowly and carefully down the road below. He looked very unsteady on his skis.

Mrs Pepperpot opened the window and called to him:

'Hi there! Come up here a minute.'

The little fellow took off his skis and climbed up the hill. Mrs Pepperpot met him in the door.

'D'you like fresh-baked bread with butter and honey on it?' she asked.

'Oh yes, please,' said the boy.

'Well, come on in and sit down. I'll have a cup of coffee at the same time.'

While he munched the bread and honey, Mrs Pepperpot asked him his name.

'Arne,' he said.

'Why weren't you up on the slope, skiing with the others, Arne?' she asked.

''Cos I'm not very good at it,' said Arne, looking at her sadly, 'and the others tease me and call me a cowardy custard. They say I'm afraid of the moose up there in the pine trees and a lot of other stuff. They don't like me!'

He wiped a hand over his eyes and gave a little sniff.

'Don't you worry, Arne,' said Mrs Pepperpot, 'I won't call you a coward,' and she put an arm round his shoulders.

'This is my first winter in the snow. Before that, I lived in France with my mum and dad.'

'No wonder you're new to skiing then!' said Mrs Pepperpot. 'D'you know, when I was a little girl I was very afraid to go down those steep slopes. But I found a way to get over it.'

Arne was looking at her eagerly now: 'What did you do?'

'You'll laugh when you hear,' said Mrs

Pepperpot. 'I took my mother's old dough trough – the very same one I've been using today to make the bread. Look, it's got nice high sides to stop you falling out, and I took it up to the top of that slope and rode down in it. In fact, it was such fun I wouldn't mind doing it again.'

'Weren't you frightened after that?'

'Never again,' said Mrs Pepperpot. 'If you like, we could try it together, because I have another trough as well.'

Arne looked doubtful.

'I don't know – people might see us . . .'

'Not if we get up very early in the morning and go up to the top before anyone else is about.'

So Arne agreed and next day, when the sun rose, he and Mrs Pepperpot set off, each with a dough trough under their arm. They walked right to the top of the higher slope, where the row of pine trees cast a shadow on the hard glistening snow.

'I hope no one saw us,' said Arne, who kept looking back over his shoulder.

'Of course not,' said Mrs Pepperpot, 'all

those big boys will be snoring their heads off at this time of day.'

But Arne was still nervous: 'Have you ever seen a moose come out of those trees?'

'Bless you, yes, but he knows me, and he won't bother us, I promise you,' said Mrs Pepperpot.

'I think I'll go first!' said Arne, as he settled himself in the dough trough.

'Off you go, then!' said Mrs Pepperpot and gave him a good push to start him off.

Arne shot down the slope. The wooden trough churned up the snow; it blew in his eyes, so that he had to close them, and he couldn't see where he was going. But he didn't mind, because there were no obstacles in the way and he was holding on to the sides very tightly. In fact, he was really enjoying the ride. That is, till the trough stopped and he opened his eyes.

There, on either side of him, stood the whole crowd of boys from his class!

'Here comes the champion tobogganer!' shouted one, and they all roared with laughter.

'The very latest design!' jeered another.

'What did you do with the old woman? Isn't she coming down in her trough too? Or perhaps she's even more scared than you are . . .'

And so they went on, while poor Arne wished he could bury himself in the snow and that Mrs Pepperpot would not appear.

From the top of the slope Mrs Pepperpot had seen the boys arrive. She was just wondering what to do, when she SHRANK!

For once she was not too sorry to be tiny. At least the boys wouldn't see her. She would just sit in her trough and wait till they went away.

But at that moment the bull moose came ambling out of the pine trees. 'Hi, Moose!' shouted Mrs Pepperpot from the trough.

The big animal came over and blew hot air on Mrs Pepperpot through his huge nostrils: 'What's the trouble this time, Mrs Pepperpot?' he asked.

'Well,' she said, 'I've had an idea, and if you'll help me today, maybe I can do you a good turn another time.'

'Ho, ho,' he chuckled, 'what could a little lady like you do for me?'

'You'll be surprised,' she answered, and then she told him her plan: he was to sit in the big trough and slide down the slope to where the group of boys were standing. The last part of the plan she whispered in his ear, and then she gave him a good push and away he went.

Well, that big bull moose had the greatest difficulty in keeping his balance in the wooden trough, but he managed not to fall off till it came to a standstill at the place where the boys stood – or rather *had* stood. For they had seen him coming and had scattered in every direction as fast as they could go.

All except poor Arne, who was standing there with his trough. His eyes were filled with tears, so he didn't see anything till the moose came to rest right next to him.

As the huge beast got to his feet, Arne was too frightened to move. But the moose took a step towards him and then did something which made all the boys stare: with his big thick tongue he licked Arne's face!

Arne was no longer frightened; he could tell the moose was friendly. He put his hand up to the big head and stroked his ears. Then the moose quietly ambled back to the slope and disappeared in the trees.

And Mrs Pepperpot? Well, she appeared on the scene, as large as life, just as those boys came edging up to shake Arne by the hand.

'He's a brave boy, isn't he?' she said, putting her arm round Arne's shoulder. 'Who'd have thought such a little fellow could tame that old bull moose?'

Spring cleaning

IT WAS a beautiful day in March. The sun was doing its best to melt the last remaining snow-drifts and cast a glow over the tall pine trees on the mountain ridge. Everything suddenly looked sharper and clearer in outline. Even the wooden walls of Mrs Pepperpot's house seemed to shine like polished tin. But when she looked at her windows she didn't thank the sun; it showed up how very dirty they were.

'Oh dear,' she said to herself. 'I can see it's time for spring-cleaning again. Well, I might as well get down to it straight away, I suppose.'

She went into the kitchen to get out her bucket, her scrubbing brush and plenty of soap and scouring powder. Mrs Pepperpot was pretty thorough when she got going – in fact, she enjoyed spring-cleaning.

She was just about to start on the windows

when she heard a slow buzzing sound over by the stove. A big black fly had come out of the corner where it had been sleeping.

'Oho!' she said, 'so the sun's woken you up too, has it? Well, you needn't think I'm letting you lay eggs all over my house, making millions of flies to blacken my windows in the summer. I'll fix you!' and she rushed at the fly with a fly-swatter.

But the fly got away, because at that moment Mrs Pepperpot SHRANK!

'You wait!' she shrilled in her tiny voice, as she rolled along the floor, 'I'll get you!'

'Don't worry,' said a voice from the corner.

Mrs Pepperpot turned round; it was a large spider hanging by its thread from a web it had spun between the grandfather clock and the wall.

'Don't worry,' said the spider, 'I'll deal with that pest.'

'You gave me quite a fright!' said Mrs Pepperpot, 'I don't mean to be rude, but I've never seen you so close to before, and I didn't know you were so hairy and ugly . . .'

'I could return the compliment,' said the

spider, 'but on the whole you look a bit better when you're small than when you're tramping round the kitchen in your great big shoes. Anyway, did you hear me offer to catch that fat fly for you?'

'Yes, I did,' answered Mrs Pepperpot, 'but I certainly wouldn't let you roll that poor creature up in your horrible web to be eaten for breakfast. No, indeed. If I had seen that contraption of yours before I shrank, I would have whisked it away with my broom!'

'Leave it to me!' said another little voice right behind her. This time it was a mouse.

'It's you, is it? And what d'you think a little scrap like you can do?' asked Mrs Pepperpot scornfully.

'Who's talking?' squeaked the mouse cheek-ily, 'you're not exactly outsize yourself at the moment. At least *I* can run up the clock – dickory, dickory dock!' he laughed. 'And then I can snip that web with my sharp teeth as easy as winking!'

'I'm sure you can,' said Mrs Pepperpot, 'but don't you see? That web is the spider's liveli-hood. Without those threads she couldn't catch her food and she would die.'

'Well, in that case,' said the mouse, 'I sup-pose you're supplying me with *my* livelihood when you leave the cover off the cheese dish in the larder, hee, hee!'

'You little thief!' shouted Mrs Pepperpot, shaking her tiny fist at the mouse. 'You push it off yourself, you and your wretched family. But I'll set a trap for you this very evening!'

'Did I hear a mouse?' asked another voice from the door. It was the cat. 'Where is it? I'm just ready for my dinner.'

'No, no!' shrieked Mrs Pepperpot, waving her arms at the cat, while the mouse was trying to hide behind her skirt. 'You leave the mouse alone, you great brute, you. He hasn't done you any harm, has he?'

'Woof! Woof! Who's a brute round here?' The head of a strange dog was peering round the door. When he caught sight of the cat he darted after her, knocking Mrs Pepperpot over as he ran round the table.

The cat managed to get out of the door with the dog close behind her when, luckily, at that moment Mrs Pepperpot grew to her normal size! She lost no time in throwing a stick at the dog while Pussy jumped on to the shed roof. The dog went on barking till Mrs Pepperpot gave him a bone. Then he trotted off down the hill.

'Dear me, what a to-do!' thought Mrs Pepperpot, 'but it makes you wonder; every little creature is hunted by a bigger creature who in turn is hunted by a bigger one. Where does it all end?'

'Right here!' said a deep voice behind her.

Mrs Pepperpot nearly jumped out of her skin, but when she turned round it was her husband standing there.

'Oh,' she said, 'I thought you were an ogre come to gobble me up!'

'Well!' said Mr Pepperpot. 'Is that all the

thanks I get for coming home early to help with the spring-cleaning?'

'You darling man!' said Mrs Pepperpot, giving him a great big kiss.

Easter chicks

EVERY YEAR when it gets near Easter time and the shop windows are full of fluffy cotton wool Easter chicks, Mrs Pepperpot sends a message to the children round about that she would like them to do her shopping for her. The children are only too pleased, because Mrs Pepperpot always gives them sweets, and sometimes even money to spend on themselves. So there is often quite a queue outside her door. But as soon as Easter is over and those yellow chicks disappear from the window displays, Mrs Pepperpot starts to do her shopping herself again.

Now why does the little old woman behave in this peculiar way? I'll tell you.

One Easter, many years ago, Mrs Pepperpot got it into her head that she wanted to rear chickens. She could have bought day-old chicks from a hatchery, but no:

'Chickens need a mother!' she declared.

So she went to a neighbour and borrowed a broody hen. Not all hens want to rear chicks; some spend their time preening their feathers, looking for food and laying their eggs wherever a box is handy. But a broody hen starts to collect her eggs in one nest and gets all hot and bothered if anyone tries to take them away.

The neighbour put the whole nest with ten eggs in a carton and the broody hen on top, and Mrs Pepperpot carried it home very carefully. She had already prepared a corner of her sitting-room with a little curtain across to keep out the draught, and the hen settled down very nicely.

Mr Pepperpot was not pleased: 'Proper place for a hen is in the out-house,' he said. But every time he went near the broody hen to take her out, she pecked and squawked so much, he had to give it up.

Every day Mrs Pepperpot lifted the curtain and peeped in to see if the hen was all right. She brought her water and some grain, but the hen was not very interested in eating or drinking. She just sat there, keeping the eggs warm.

The day came when the hatching should begin.

Mrs Pepperpot walked round the house, singing. She was so excited, she couldn't keep still, and every so often she went over to the corner and crouched down to listen.

'Those little chicks should be pecking their way out of their shells any minute now,' she told herself.

And then she heard an unmistakable sound: 'Cheep, cheep!' it said, very faintly.

Immediately the mother hen started clucking and fussing. Soon there were more cheeps, until at last the mother hen strutted out from behind the curtain, followed by nine little golden chicks.

Mrs Pepperpot clapped her hands with joy as she watched them following their mother. Then she knelt down to see what had happened to the tenth egg.

It was still lying in the nest, quite smooth and whole among all the broken shells.

'Oh, you poor little thing,' said Mrs Pepperpot. 'Perhaps you need some help with that

hard shell . . .' But as she stretched out her hand
to pick it up, she SHRANK!

She not only found herself lying in the nest by
the egg, but there was a great shadow towering
over her – Mother Hen!

'Don't peck me!' she cried, because the hen

looked very fierce, 'I was only trying to help your last chick out of the egg.'

The hen opened her beak and squawked at her. It sounded something like: *'Fi fi, finicula!'*

'Now listen!' said Mrs Pepperpot, trying to dodge Mother Hen's flapping wings, 'I'm Mrs Pepperpot – you know – the old woman who shrinks, and I understand animal and bird language – but I don't know what you're talking about.'

The hen just went on squawking and gabbling her strange nonsense: *'Fi fi finicula, ratagusa balla tella!'*

'Will you listen a minute!' Mrs Pepperpot was losing patience; 'I'm not trying to hurt your chicks. You just take them for a nice walk round the room and leave me to sit here till I grow big again. Now, run along!'

The hen took no notice. She charged straight at Mrs Pepperpot and with her strong wings buffeted her right out of the nest on to the mat where all the baby chicks were darting about and cheeping their heads off.

'What a din!' said Mrs Pepperpot, scrambling to her feet and trying to keep out of the way.

Mother Hen now turned her attention to her family. Clucking in a commanding tone, she chivvied them into line and made them follow behind her as she walked slowly across the room.

Mrs Pepperpot stood watching the wonderful way the chicks obeyed her, when suddenly Mother Hen turned round and saw her there.

'*Seguira linia malachita*' she squawked and rushed at her, pecking at Mrs Pepperpot's hair.

'Ouch!' shouted Mrs Pepperpot. 'What d'you think you're doing? I'm not one of your children!'

The only reply she got was more gibberish and more angry pecks. So, to avoid being pecked to pieces, she fell into line and followed Mother Hen till they came to the spot where Mrs Pepperpot had strewn some fine oatmeal for the baby chicks to eat.

Mother Hen stopped and clucked to the chicks to gather round. Then she showed them how to pick up the meal and soon they all had their heads down, their beaks sounding like tiny drums on the floor. Mrs Pepperpot had to laugh as she watched them, but not for long, because Mother Hen was after her again:

'*Mangiamello, mangiamello!*' and more pecks rained on the little old woman's head.

'Stop! Stop!' she yelled. 'I don't know what you're saying, but I'll have some oatmeal, if that's what you want.'

She picked some up in her hand and pre-tended to put it in her mouth.

'*Uccella stupida*,' scolded the hen, flapping her with a wing.

'Oh very well, you silly old fuss-pot!' said Mrs Pepperpot, and she got down on all fours and pretended to peck at the oatmeal with her nose.

When the baby chicks had had enough, Mother Hen led them over to a pan of water which Mrs Pepperpot had put there for them. Mother Hen showed them how to drink, dipping their beaks and then putting their heads well back.

'Drink like a hen? That's one thing you're not going to get me to do, madam!' declared Mrs Pepperpot.

'*Bere, bere!*' squawked the hen swooping on her so hard that she fell right into the pan of water.

The next moment she was back to her normal size and standing there with her wet clothes dripping on to the sitting-room floor.

'You're worse than my teacher at school!' said Mrs Pepperpot, rubbing her sore head.

The hen was now behaving very strangely, fluttering to and fro and calling anxiously.

'What's the matter?' said Mrs Pepperpot, 'looking for your lost chick?' and she went over to the nest and picked up the tenth egg. She broke the shell, but there was no chick inside.

'I'm afraid you'll have to do with nine,' she

said, 'as I'm not following a hen around who doesn't even speak my language. Whoever heard of a bird that can't understand Mrs Pepperpot when she shrinks?'

'*Mi scusi!*' clucked the hen.

And suddenly Mrs Pepperpot understood what had happened. The hen was an Italian Leghorn and she was talking hen Italian!

The mystery was solved, and you would think Mrs Pepperpot would be satisfied. But she never got over the shock of having to be a baby chick and doing what she was told by Mother Hen.

So that's why she won't even look at those fluffy yellow Easter chicks in the shop window.

The cuckoo

IN MAY, when the first green veil of leaves covers the birch trees and the wagtail starts to follow the plough, that is the time for the cuckoo to arrive.

Mrs Pepperpot was just locking her door to go to the shop when she heard it:

'Cuckoo!'

'Cuckoo!' answered Mrs Pepperpot, but she didn't say it very loudly, in case the cuckoo might get annoyed. For Mrs Pepperpot is a little afraid of the cuckoo. It can bring good luck, but it can also bring you bad luck. It depends from which direction you hear it calling.

Mrs Pepperpot looked all around her, but couldn't see where the bird was sitting.

'Cuckoo!'

There it was again, and this time she was sure she heard it from the west.

'"Cuckoo from the west, all for the best!"' she chanted, and went on her way down the hill, quite content. But soon she stopped, and a frightened look came over her face. What if her husband had heard the same bird? He would have heard it from the north, for he was working on the road down in the valley.

'Oh dear!' she said, '"Cuckoo from the north, sorrow bring forth!"'

At that moment she SHRANK! and found herself sitting on the ground under a high pine tree. Up above she could hear the angry noise of her friend, the squirrel.

She called to him: 'Hi, squirrel! Could you come down here, please!'

'Chuck! Chuck!' he scolded, running down the tree trunk head first. 'What's up with Mrs Pepperpot this time? You look very woe-be-gone.'

'Well, it's my husband, you see,' said Mrs Pepperpot, 'I'm afraid he'll have heard the cuckoo from the north, and that means bad luck for him.'

'Chuck! Just the sort of thing an old woman

like you would worry about! What d'you want *me* to do about it?'

'I thought you might take me up to the top of the tree, so that I could talk to the cuckoo, and perhaps get him to call from the east. "Cuckoo from the east, harbingers a feast," you see.'

'Rubbish,' said the squirrel. 'But hurry up now. I've got better things to do than carry superstitious old women around!'

'So I notice!' said Mrs Pepperpot. 'There's egg-yolk round your nose.'

The squirrel's tail switched angrily. 'It's none of your business what I have for breakfast! Are you ready?' and he scuttled up to the top of the tall pine tree with Mrs Pepperpot.

Once up there, Mrs Pepperpot clung to a small branch. It made her giddy to look down.

'Bye, bye!' said the squirrel. 'I hope the cuckoo doesn't keep you waiting too long!'

'You're not going to leave me up here all alone, are you?' said poor Mrs Pepperpot.

'You silly woman! The cuckoo won't come near you if I'm here. I'll fetch you later.' And with that he was off.

Mrs Pepperpot's arms were quite stiff with holding on before the cuckoo finally alighted in the tree. He was a little surprised to find her there. 'Did you fall out of an aeroplane?' he asked.

'No, Mr Cuckoo,' said Mrs Pepperpot politely, 'I came up here to speak to you.'

'I'm a little busy just now...' said the cuckoo, opening his beak to call again.

'Stop, please!' cried Mrs Pepperpot.

The cuckoo shut his beak and looked at her in astonishment.

'Mr Cuckoo, will you do me a big favour?' she pleaded. 'Will you fly over to the east side of the valley and call from there?'

'Why should I?' said the cuckoo, 'I'm calling to my wife and she's on this side of the valley.'

'It'll bring good luck to my husband if you do. He's working down there on the road.'

The cuckoo looked flattered: 'Oh well, if you put it that way, of course I'll oblige.' And he flew off straight away.

A little while later Mrs Pepperpot heard him:

'Cuckoo!' he called and it sounded such a happy note, she was sure it would cheer her husband up.

Then she remembered she hadn't done her shopping yet, and Mr Pepperpot would be expecting a feast when he got home!

'Oh dear! Now what shall I do?' she wailed.

At that moment the squirrel reappeared.

'You moaning again?' he said. 'I'll have to get that cuckoo to sing to you from the south; "Cuckoo from the south will button up your mouth!"' he chuckled.

'That's enough of your cheek!' said Mrs Pepperpot, 'kindly get me down to earth at once!'

It was not a minute too soon. As her feet touched the ground she grew large again. She waved good-bye to the squirrel, picked up her basket and hurried to the shop.

When she came back she had bought her husband's favourite sausages and two pounds of macaroni, and for pudding she set to work making pancakes with bilberry jam. Then she laid the table with her good china and put a lighted candle in the middle.

'Hullo, hullo!' said Mr Pepperpot when he came in. 'Whose birthday?'

'Didn't you hear the cuckoo?' she asked anxiously.

'What cuckoo?' Mr Pepperpot looked puzzled.

'You mean to say you didn't hear it either from the north or from the east?'

'Good lord, no,' said Mr Pepperpot. 'Much too busy with that mechanical digger; blasts your ear-drums, it does, all day!'

Just then they *both* heard the cuckoo, and this time it was right over their heads on the roof!

'That's the best luck of all!' cried Mrs Pepperpot, giving her husband a big kiss. 'Now we really can enjoy our feast!'

Midsummer romance

IN NORWAY at Midsummer the sun hardly sets at all, and at night the sky is almost as bright as during the day. So how do people get to sleep? If they're young and gay they don't bother; they stay up and dance round a bonfire on Midsummer Eve or go for long romantic walks in the woods till they can't keep their eyes open any longer, light or no light.

But Mrs Pepperpot's dancing days are over; this Midsummer Eve she decided to take a walk through the wood to visit Miss Flora Bundy, a spinster lady who lived by herself in a little cottage. Miss Flora was shy and timid and had hardly any friends to visit her, so Mrs Pepperpot thought she would cheer her up with some home-made cakes and a bottle of home-made wine.

'I feel like Little Red Riding Hood,' she thought, as she walked through the shadowy wood with her basket on her arm. 'I hope I don't meet that old wolf on the way.'

But she arrived at the cottage quite safely and knocked on the door. There was no answer. After she had knocked three times she tried the door and found it unlocked, so she went in.

'Are you there, Miss Flora?' she called.

Still silence. So she put her basket down in the hall and walked through the little sitting-room to the bedroom.

'No wolf in the bed, anyway!' she said, looking down at it. But what was that? Arranged across the pillow was a row of wild flowers – each of a different kind. Tears came into Mrs Pepperpot's eyes:

'Who would have believed it?' she said. 'Miss Flora collecting wild flowers to put under her pillow on Midsummer's Eve so that she will dream about the man she will marry. How very romantic!'

Then she looked again. There were only eight flowers; to make the dream come true, there should be nine different wild flowers.

'Of course!' she said. 'She's out looking for the ninth one.'

And, sure enough, when she looked through the window, there was Miss Flora walking up the path very slowly, her eyes fixed on the ground.

Mrs Pepperpot was just wondering how to explain her being in Miss Flora's bedroom, when she SHRANK!

Quick as lightning, she grabbed the edge of the sheet and climbed up, hand over hand, till she reached the pillow. Then she slipped in under it and lay still as a mouse.

Miss Flora came in and sat down on the chair by the window. As lonely people often do, she talked aloud to herself:

'It looks as if I won't find that ninth flower again this year. Ah well, perhaps it's all for the best! It would be dreadful if I dreamed about anyone else but the dear postman!'

'The postman, eh?' muttered Mrs Pepperpot under the pillow. 'If anything, he's more shy than Miss Flora!'

'I'll just count the flowers once more,' said

Miss Flora, when she had changed into her nightdress and was ready to get into bed.

Slowly she began to count: 'cornflower one, buttercup two, cowslip three, bluebell four, dandelion five, wild rose six, honeysuckle seven, poppy eight, cornflower nine.'

Did you notice? Miss Flora counted the cornflower twice. But *she* didn't notice that Mrs Pepperpot had put out her tiny hand from underneath the pillow and popped the cornflower from the beginning of the row to the other end!

Miss Flora clapped her hands and snatched up the flowers:

'There *are* nine. Hooray! Now I will go to sleep and dream about the man I love.' And she tucked the little posy under the pillow – right next to where Mrs Pepperpot was lying!

When Miss Flora had gone to sleep, Mrs Pepperpot eased herself from under the pillow and slid gently down the side of the bed on to the writing-table by the window.

As I told you, it was not really dark at all, so she quickly found a piece of paper and a pen. Being so small, she had some difficulty in holding the pen and writing the words large enough. But she managed it at last. Then she found a pink envelope and put the note inside. She wrote some more words across the front. Then she stood in the open window and gave a little whistle.

The sound was heard by a swallow in her nest under the eaves.

'I know who that is,' said the swallow, swooping down on to the window-sill. 'At your service, Mrs Pepperpot!'

'Thank you, Swallow,' said the little old woman, holding out the envelope. 'Will you please take this to the postman's house? But make sure he sees it, even if you have to wake him up with a peck on his nose!'

'No sooner said than done,' said the swallow and was gone.

Mrs Pepperpot sat on the window-sill, swinging her little legs and enjoying the warm night air. It wasn't long before the bird was back.

'Did you deliver the letter?' asked Mrs Pepperpot.

'Yes,' laughed the swallow. 'You should have seen the postman jump out of bed when I pecked his nose; he must have thought a wasp stung him!'

'But did he read what it said on the envelope?'

'He did. And I left him pulling on his trousers as he rushed out to get his bicycle. He should be on his way.'

'Good, good. My plot is working very well!' said Mrs Pepperpot, and thanked the swallow for her help.

Then she sat down again to watch how things turned out.

But a postman on a bicycle takes much longer

than a swallow on the wing to get from the village to the cottage in the wood, and Mrs Pepperpot was almost out of patience when he arrived, puffing a little from pedalling so hard. He was a tall, thin man who usually wore a sad expression on his face. This was because he was lonely and had no one to care for him at home.

Now, as he stood in front of the little cottage, Mrs Pepperpot could see he was smiling.

'At last!' he said. 'For years I've waited for this chance to visit dear Miss Flora. And now perhaps I can bring her good news this Midsummer morning.'

So Miss Flora had never had a letter delivered before? thought Mrs Pepperpot: 'The poor lady! Won't she be surprised?'

The postman went up to the door and gave first a timid knock, then a louder one. He was just about to knock for the third time, when the door opened, and there stood Miss Flora in a pretty flowered dressing gown.

'Oh!' she gasped. 'Is it really you, Postman?'

'I've brought you this letter,' he said, holding out the pink envelope.

'For me?' Miss Flora looked very surprised. 'Who can have written to me?' And she opened the letter then and there.

The postman waited while she read it: 'I hope it brings good news?'

'How strange,' she said. 'Just one line: "Congratulations and best wishes from the queen of the flowers".'

Peeping from behind a flower-pot on the window-sill, Mrs Pepperpot now saw the postman kneel on one knee in the dewy grass and heard him say:

'Dearest Miss Flora, to me *you* are the queen of the flowers!'

And what did Miss Flora do? She kissed her dear postman and they went indoors, hand in hand.

At the same moment, Mrs Pepperpot fell off the window-sill and grew to her normal size.

'Well,' she said to herself, as she walked home. 'That was a good Midsummer night's work. I hope they find the cakes and wine for their celebration.'

Mrs Pepperpot and the pedlar

IN AUGUST Mrs Pepperpot's garden was full of bright dahlias and asters and marigolds. They made her feel so cheerful, she decided to put on her new blue and yellow striped skirt with a clean white blouse, fastened at the neck with a red brooch.

From the oven came the delicious smell of a ginger cake she was baking, and she was just about to put on the coffee-pot, when a shadow passed across the window.

Before he had time to knock on the door, Mrs Pepperpot saw who it was. She rushed to the cupboard and pulled out an old black shawl and threw it round her shoulders. It hung well down over her striped skirt and when she had mussed up her hair and looked really miserable, she went to the door and opened it.

'Come in,' she said in a funny old granny

voice, and in walked the person she least wanted to see that day, Mr Trick. A travelling salesman he called himself, but he was more like an old-fashioned pedlar, he had so many different things in his suitcase. He had the knack of calling just when Mrs Pepperpot had managed to save up a little money (which she kept in a cracked blue cup), and by the time he left she had always somehow spent every penny.

'Hullo, hullo, hullo!' he greeted her loudly. 'Are we doing a little business today?'

'How can a poor old woman like me do business?' she asked in that squeaky voice. 'Where would I get the money from?'

'Got it all safely stashed in the bank, I suppose,' laughed Mr Trick. 'Not like me, never make enough to put in the bank. All I get from some people are kisses and promises.'

Mrs Pepperpot had to laugh at his cheek, and soon there she was, rummaging through his open suitcase and picking out useless things like cotton ribbon and a coffee strainer, though she had two already. Meanwhile Mr Trick went on talking about banks:

'No, I don't believe in them; make it a point of honour never to have a bank book.'

'*I* make it a point of honour never to burn a cake,' said Mrs Pepperpot. 'So I'd better go and see if it's done.'

'Allow me, Mrs Pepperpot,' said Mr Trick, 'I'm an expert on baking. I will inspect your cake while you go on inspecting my goods.' And he went out into the kitchen.

Mrs Pepperpot went on rummaging, and at the back of the suitcase she found a secret pocket. There was a book in it, and when she pulled it out she saw it was a bank book with Mr Trick's name inside!

'No bank book, indeed! I'll teach you a lesson, Mr Smart Alec Trick.' And she hid the book behind the curtain. But when she turned back to the suitcase, she SHRANK and tumbled in among the hankies, socks and other fancy goods.

When Mr Trick came back he was surprised not to find her and called out her name a couple of times. But then he closed the suitcase and seemed in a hurry to leave. He strapped it on the back of his moped, and soon poor Mrs Pepperpot was having a very bumpy ride along the main road to the next town. There Mr Trick took the suitcase with him into the biggest bank and opened it on the counter.

Luckily he was talking to the cashier when Mrs Pepperpot sneaked out of the case and hid behind some forms on the counter. Because now he started looking for that bank book and had everything out of the case in his frantic search.

'What can I have done with it?' he wailed. 'I want to pay in some more money, and I'm sure I put the bank book in my case when I left home.'

The cashier told him he could just sign a piece of paper to show how much he was paying in, and Mr Trick pulled out lots and lots of notes from his inner pocket. Last of all he counted out some small coins; they came to exactly the amount that Mrs Pepperpot had saved in the cracked blue cup at home!

'Well!' said Mrs Pepperpot to herself. 'You not only tell lies, but steal a poor woman's savings! If I was my right size I'd call the police.'

But she was still tiny, so what could she do? She puzzled for a moment, then she hit on an idea. Pulling out one of the forms from its holder, she dipped her finger in the ink-stand and wrote as large as she could:

'Your bank book has been found at Mrs Pepperpot's. Please fetch it at once.'

She pushed the piece of paper along the counter, so that Mr Trick would see it when he stopped chatting to the cashier.

'What an extraordinary thing!' said Mr Trick when he read it. 'Someone must have telephoned.'

While he and the cashier were trying to work this out, Mrs Pepperpot slipped back in the suitcase and was relieved when it was picked up and strapped on to the moped again. Off they went on the bumpy road back to Mrs Pepperpot's house. When they got there Mr Trick rushed straight to the door. As he knocked, there was the most terrific bang! He looked back and there stood Mrs Pepperpot, as large as life, beside his moped with the contents of his suitcase strewn all over the hillside!

'D'you keep bombs in your case?' she asked innocently, as she came forward to open the door.

'Certainly not!' said Mr Trick, who looked very uncomfortable. 'I had a message about a book I had left . . .'

'A *bank* book, Mr Trick,' said Mrs Pepperpot, 'with your name clearly on the inside.'

'Well, yes . . .' he answered, 'of course, it was my little joke about not using banks . . .'

'Your joke, too, I suppose, to take a poor old woman's savings from a cracked blue cup?' And she went over and turned the cup upside down. It was empty.

'I can explain – honestly I can!' Mr Trick was talking very fast now; 'I took the cake out of the oven and put it on the table. Then I saw the money and was bringing it in for you to pay me for the goods you chose and then you'd disappeared!'

'A likely story! I ought to call the police and show you up for the menace you are to poor old women like me. Now give me my money and be off before I change my mind.'

With a trembling hand, Mr Trick counted out the money he had stolen and was just about to slink off, when Mrs Pepperpot called him back.

'You've forgotten something,' she said and handed him his bank book.

The moose hunt

THERE'S ONE week in the year that Mrs Pepperpot hates: that's the first week in October when people with guns are allowed to shoot the moose. All the rest of the year the big animals roam in the forest as they like and nobody hurts them.

Mrs Pepperpot had her special friend, the big bull moose, and in the summer she was always running down to the stream at the edge of the forest with cabbage leaves or lettuce for him. In winter during the snow she put down great armfuls of hay. So neither the big bull moose nor his friends and relations ran away when they saw her coming.

But as the time came near for the shooting to begin, Mrs Pepperpot got more and more agitated. How could she warn the moose not to come out in the open, but to stay hidden deep in the forest?

Several days before the hunt she stopped taking green stuff down to the place where she usually fed them. Instead she took a dustbin lid and a wooden ladle and stood there, banging away and shouting as loud as she could to frighten the animals away.

Then came the night before the hunt and Mrs Pepperpot was walking up and down in her sitting-room, wringing her hands.

Mr Pepperpot took no notice; he was very proud of the fact that he had been asked to take part in the hunt with two local bigwigs, Mr Rich, the landowner, and Mr Packer, the chain-store grocer. They would be coming to fetch him early in the morning, and Mr Pepperpot was busy getting his green felt hat and jacket ready.

'How can you be so heartless and cruel?' asked Mrs Pepperpot tearfully.

'Nonsense, wife,' he answered. 'The hunt only goes on for ten days and only a few moose get shot. After all, we can't have those great elephants tramping down all the young trees, can we? Besides, it's good sport.' And he took down his gun to give it a clean.

'They're not elephants; they're very graceful,' said Mrs Pepperpot, 'and I don't want you to kill them.'

'Well, you can't stop me,' said her husband firmly.

'We'll see about that!' she muttered and walked out into the night.

She walked quickly down the hill, but just as she had crossed the stream and gone through the gate, she SHRANK!

'For once I'm not sorry to be small!' she said, picking herself up and looking round. 'At least the animals can understand what I say now – if I can *find* any animals.'

She started calling: 'Any moose about? Mooooose! Can you hear me?'

But it was so dark and her voice was so small and thin that no moose either saw or heard her.

But one creature did; her faithful friend, the squirrel. He happened to be sitting in the tree above her.

'What are you yelling for?' he asked and scuttled down the tree.

'Oh squirrel, thank goodness you've come,'

said Mrs Pepperpot. 'You must help me warn the moose. They mustn't come out in the open, for tomorrow the men will be there with their guns and will shoot them.'

'Right,' said the squirrel, 'I'll get my bush telegraph into action and send messages to as many as I can.'

'Thank you!' said Mrs Pepperpot, 'I knew you would help. But there's more to be done; I have a plan to foil those evil huntsmen. Bend down and I'll whisper it to you.'

The two of them whispered together for a long time before Mrs Pepperpot grew large again and the squirrel scuttled away to carry out the plan.

Mrs Pepperpot went home; now she could sleep with a quiet mind. In the morning her husband thought she must have come to her senses at last, for there she was on the doorstep with him, ready to greet the smart hunters with their picnic baskets and expensive guns and dogs.

Mrs Pepperpot was a little surprised to see Mrs Rich there as well, all dressed up in check trousers and a big feather in her hat. But she smiled at her too, and wished them all a good day's hunting as they left.

Then Mrs Pepperpot went shopping. On her way down she met Nora North, who said:

'Fancy seeing you out today. I thought you'd be sitting at home crying your eyes out for the poor moose.'

Mrs Pepperpot put on a solemn face and answered: 'Yes, it's a sad day for me and all animal lovers. But there we are, I can't change the law, so what's the good of moping?'

In the shop Mrs Pepperpot went to the counter selling toilet goods and first aid things. She bought a good length of bandage, some splints and plenty of soothing ointment and witchhazel. The sales lady asked if Mr Pepperpot had had an accident.

'Oh, no,' said Mrs Pepperpot, 'but it's just as well to be prepared.' Then she went home again and waited.

Bang! A distant shot rang out.

'Oh dear!' said Mrs Pepperpot, covering her ears with her hands, 'I hope that was a miss.'

She went outside and stared anxiously in the direction of the forest. Wasn't that someone coming out of the gate? It *was*, followed by a sad-looking dog.

Mrs Pepperpot waited while the person slowly climbed the hill. When he got nearer she could see it was Mr Packer, but he was limping and supporting himself on a stick!

'Why, whatever happened to you, Mr Packer?' she cried.

'Oh, it was terrible!' moaned Mr Packer. 'My dog here had just got a good scent and I was ready with my gun as soon as a moose came in sight, when a whole flock of grouse came whirring out of the undergrowth and flew right at me! They knocked my hat and my glasses off and I ran into a fallen tree, giving myself the most awful bump. I'm sure my leg is broken!'

'Poor Mr Packer!' said Mrs Pepperpot, helping him indoors. 'Let's have a look at your leg.'

It turned out not to be broken, but Mrs Pepperpot put the splints on all the same and

bandaged it so tightly, the poor man could hardly move.

Next to arrive was Mr Rich. You never saw such a sight! Not just his hat was green now; he was covered in grassy green slush from head to foot.

His dog had picked up a good scent which led them along the edge of a small bog in a glade; when suddenly a squirrel leaped clean out of the top of a tree on to Mr Rich's head, causing him to lose his balance and topple into the bog.

'I might have been drowned!' he wailed,

squelching through the front door into the kitchen. There, curiously enough, Mrs Pepperpot had a big tub of hot water waiting, complete with a towel and dry underwear for just such an emergency. But Mr Rich was too wet and miserable to ask any questions.

'I hope nothing has happened to Mrs Rich and my husband,' said Mrs Pepperpot, looking quite concerned. They didn't have long to wait before the two of them came up the hill, holding hands and groping their way, as if they were blind. Which they were, almost. For they had walked into a swarm of bees and their faces were quite swollen with stings.

'Oh, you poor, poor things!' cried Mrs Pepperpot, 'how lucky I have some witchhazel!' And she set to work dabbing their faces and making hot cups of coffee for everyone.

'Blest if I even heard those bees coming!' grumbled Mr Pepperpot, when the rest of the party had gone home.

'God's creatures work in a mysterious way,' smiled Mrs Pepperpot, 'and I don't mean only the human kind!'

Mr Pepperpot and the weather

MRS PEPPERPOT never listens to weather reports.

'If the sun shines I'm glad; if it rains I stay indoors,' she says.

But Mr Pepperpot listens to every single weather report both on TV and radio. He nods wisely when they talk about depressions over Dogger Bank or when the man on TV pushes arrows around to show where the troughs of high pressure are moving to.

'Just as I thought,' said Mr Pepperpot.

Not only that; he also remembered all the old country sayings about the weather, and all the traditional signs and portents. It wouldn't matter so much, thought Mrs Pepperpot, if he didn't always look for signs of *bad* weather. If Mr Pepperpot saw a holly tree full of red berries, he was sure the winter would be hard. If he heard thunder in September that meant storms at sea.

'More likely to be rats in the attic that you heard!' muttered Mrs Pepperpot.

Or he would say that it was foggy and that a foggy autumn brings a frosty Christmas.

'Try cleaning your spectacles!' said Mrs Pepperpot. 'You might get a clearer view.'

She was getting sick of all this moaning about the weather, and she decided to provide Mr Pepperpot with a *good* omen for a change.

If the fruit trees bloom in October, she'd heard him say, it meant the winter would be mild.

There was only one fruit tree in Mrs Pepperpot's garden, an old apple tree right outside the sitting-room window.

'Beggars can't be choosers,' she said, and she sat down to make apple-blossom out of pink and white crepe paper. It took her all day, but at last she had a whole basketful of pretty pink and white flowers, which she hid in the outhouse.

Evening came and so did Mr Pepperpot. When she had given him his supper, Mrs

88

Pepperpot fetched the basket of blossoms and hung it on as high a branch as she could reach. Then she started to climb up the tree herself.

But, of course, the inevitable happened; she SHRANK!

Luckily, she fell into the basket which swung on the branch, but didn't break it.

'Phew!' said Mrs Pepperpot, 'this is going to be hard work. If it had been daytime, I could

have got the squirrel or the crow to help me; now I shall have to manage myself.'

Indoors Mr Pepperpot settled down in his armchair to watch TV. He had the radio on at the same time, in case he should miss any of the weather forecasts. So, while the TV was showing a film about girls in bikinis swimming in the warm South Seas under a blazing sun, the radio was telling Mr Pepperpot that a hailstorm was on its way to his area.

It was all very confusing, and Mr Pepperpot looked out of the window instead, just to see what the weather was *really* like.

What he saw made him blink; he couldn't believe his eyes! Out there in the garden the old apple tree was covered in pink and white blossom. Not only that, but more and more flowers kept appearing and they even seemed to be moving – creeping along the branches! Finally there was just one flower moving; it was climbing up the trunk of the tree, right to the topmost branch, which seemed to bend towards the flower, then bounce back with the flower attached like a cheeky little flag at the top.

Mr Pepperpot was stunned. It was a miracle! But just as he turned to call Mrs Pepperpot to come and look, there was a sound of breaking branches and twigs, ending in a dull thud, like a sack of flour hitting the ground.

Mrs Pepperpot came through the door, holding her hand on her hip and limping a little.

'Where have you been?' asked Mr Pepperpot.

'Out,' said Mrs Pepperpot.

'What were you doing?' he asked.

'Coming in,' she answered.

'D'you know what?' said Mr Pepperpot. 'The old apple tree is in flower. Just come and see!'

They both looked out. But all was dark; there was not a sign of a pink and white blossom! They had all fallen off when Mrs Pepperpot fell out of the tree.

'You must have dreamed it,' said Mrs Pepperpot.

'But I saw it as clear as I see you now!' he declared. 'And it made me feel so happy to think we were going to have a mild winter.'

'You go right on thinking that, my dear,' said

Mrs Pepperpot, 'stick to the good omens and leave the rest.'

And she went out into the garden and gathered up the paper flowers in her apron.

Mrs Pepperpot in hospital

MRS PEPPERPOT was in hospital.

Why? Well, you remember she fell out of that old apple tree when she was trying to make it blossom with paper flowers? After that her hip went on hurting for some time, so she went to the doctor, and he said she would have to go to hospital for X-rays, and stay overnight.

So there she was, in a nice clean hospital bed, lying next to a little girl called Rose who was going to have her tonsils out.

Rose was very unhappy. She was nearly seven years old, so it wouldn't do to cry, but she stuffed the sheet into her mouth and her little shoulders shook as she lay there with her back to Mrs Pepperpot.

'Can I do anything for you, pet?' she asked.

'Yes, please,' said the little girl stifling a sob. 'Could you tuck in my bedclothes?'

As Mrs Pepperpot went over to Rose's bed to tuck her up more comfortably, she SHRANK!

Rose was most surprised, because she thought the little old woman had disappeared. But Mrs Pepperpot called to her from the floor.

'I'm down here,' she shouted in her small voice.

'Goodness!' said Rose, looking over the edge of the bed. 'You must be Mrs Pepperpot!'

'Right first time!' said Mrs Pepperpot. 'And now it's your turn to help me.'

'What d'you want me to do?' Rose asked brightly, her tears quite forgotten.

'Pick me up in your hand and put me on your pillow,' said Mrs Pepperpot.

So Rose lifted her up.

'Fancy us two being in the same hospital,' she said.

'And in the same bed,' said Mrs Pepperpot, trying to make herself comfortable, but she kept slipping off the pillow.

'Haven't you got a box I could lie in?' she asked.

Rose brought out an empty chocolate box

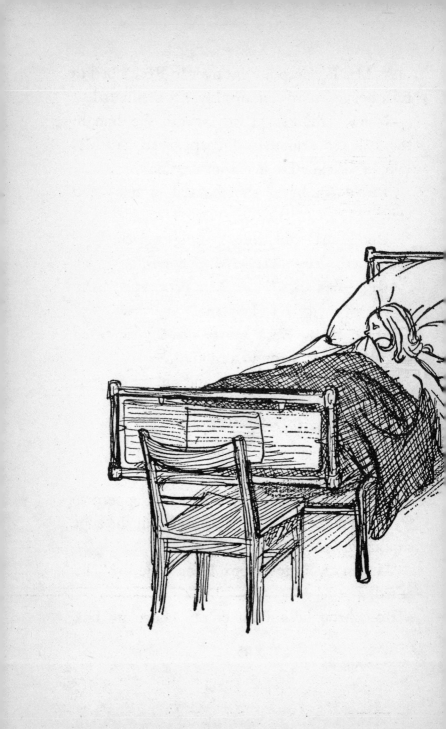

from her locker and made it up with a hankie for a sheet and her face-cloth as a coverlet.

'Now we can pretend you are my little doll,' she said. 'That was why I was sad, because I hadn't brought my doll from home. But it doesn't matter when I have you to play with.'

First they played hide and seek, with Rose shutting her eyes while Mrs Pepperpot found clever places to hide all over the bed. Then they tried 'I spy' till Rose got tired and wanted to go to sleep.

She looked sad again, and when Mrs Pepperpot asked her what was the matter, she said:

'Mummy always sings to me before I go to sleep.'

'Oh,' said Mrs Pepperpot, 'that's easy! Just wait till you hear *my* song.'

This is what she sang:

> *The Rose is white, the Rose is red,*
> *The Rose is now a sleepy-head.*
> *Soon she'll be as right as rain*
> *And play ring-a-roses with me again.*'

But then she couldn't remember any more, so

she tried to think of something else with roses:

'If Moses supposes his toeses are roses, then Moses supposes erroniousleee . . .' she began, but stopped when she saw Rose's eyes were closing.

The little girl was not quite asleep. She turned her head a bit and murmured:

'I wish my pussy was here to lick my ear – he always does that before I go to sleep at home . . .'

Mrs Pepperpot looked around, but there was not much chance of finding even the smallest kitten in a hospital ward. So she thought of another idea. She took off her woolly night-cap and dipped it in the water-glass on the table, and then she gently rubbed Rose's ear with it till she was fast asleep.

The door opened. It was the night sister coming in.

She came over to Rose's bed, but Mrs Pepperpot had popped into the chocolate box and covered herself with the face-cloth and was lying as still as any doll.

'That's one child who doesn't miss her mother,' said the night-sister, smiling down at

Rose. 'She's sleeping like an angel – and so is her dolly.'

But when she turned round and found Mrs Pepperpot's bed empty, she rushed out of the ward shouting for the doctor. In a moment she was back, followed by two doctors and two nurses, all looking for Mrs Pepperpot, who by

now, of course, had grown to her normal size and was lying in her own bed, as good as gold.

'Hullo,' said the chief doctor, 'the X-rays show your hip has mended, so you can go home tomorrow.'

'Thank you, Doctor,' said Mrs Pepperpot. 'But what about little Rose?'

'Oh,' said the doctor, 'she'll be as right as rain!' and he walked out, followed by the rest of his staff.

'And play ring-a-roses with me again,' added Mrs Pepperpot, smiling at the sleeping Rose.

Mrs Pepperpot's Christmas

ONE MORNING Mrs Pepperpot woke up and found she had shrunk. She climbed to the top of the bed-post and swung her legs while she wondered what to do.

'What a nuisance!' she said. 'Just when I wanted to go to the Christmas Market with Mr Pepperpot!'

She wanted to buy a sheaf of corn for the birds' Christmas dinner, and she wanted to get them a little bird-house where she could feed them every day. The other thing she wanted was a wreath of mistletoe to hang over the door, so that she could wish Mr Pepperpot a 'Happy Christmas' with a kiss. But Mr Pepperpot thought this was a silly idea.

'Quite unnecessary!' he said.

But Mrs Pepperpot was very clever at getting her own way; so even though she was now no bigger than a mouse, she soon worked out a plan. She heard her husband put his knapsack down on the floor in the kitchen and she slid down the bed-post, scuttled over the doorstep and climbed into one of the knapsack pockets.

Mr Pepperpot put the knapsack on his back and set off through the snow on his kick-sledge, while Mrs Pepperpot peeped out from the pocket.

'Look at all those nice cottages!' she said to herself.

'I'll bet every one of them has a sheaf of corn and a little house for the birds. And they'll have mistletoe over the door as well, no doubt. But you wait till I get home; I'll show them!'

At the market there were crowds of people, both big and small; everyone shopping, and there was plenty to choose from! At one stall stood a farmer selling beautiful golden sheaves of corn. As her husband walked past the stall Mrs Pepperpot climbed out from the knapsack pocket and disappeared inside the biggest sheaf of all.

'Hullo, Mr Pepperpot,' said the farmer, 'how

about some corn for the birds this Christmas?'

'Too dear!' answered Mr Pepperpot gruffly.

'Oh no, it's not!' squeaked the little voice of
Mrs Pepperpot.

'If you don't buy this sheaf of corn I'll tell

everyone you're married to the woman who shrinks!'

Now Mr Pepperpot above all hates people to know about his wife turning small, so when he saw her waving to him from the biggest sheaf he said to the farmer: 'I've changed my mind; I'll have that one, please!'

But the farmer told him he would have to wait in the queue.

Only a little girl saw Mrs Pepperpot slip out of the corn and dash into a bird-house on Mr Andersen's stall. He was a carpenter and made all his bird-houses look just like real little houses with doors and windows for the birds to fly in and out. Of course Mrs Pepperpot chose the prettiest house; it even had curtains in the windows and from behind these she watched her husband buy the very best sheaf of corn and stuff it in his knapsack.

He thought his wife was safe inside and was just about to get on his kick-sledge and head for home, when he heard a little voice calling from the next stall.

'Hullo, Husband!' squeaked Mrs Pepperpot.

'Haven't you forgotten something? You were going to buy me a bird-house!'

Mr Pepperpot hurried over to the stall. He pointed to the house with the curtains and said: 'I want to buy that one, please!'

Mr Andersen was busy with his customers. 'You'll have to take your turn,' he said.

So once more poor Mr Pepperpot had to stand patiently in a queue. He hoped that no one else would buy the house with his wife inside.

But she wasn't inside; she had run out of the back door, and now she was on her way to the next stall. Here there was a pretty young lady selling holly and mistletoe. Mrs Pepperpot had to climb up the post to reach the nicest wreath, and there she stayed hidden.

Soon Mr Pepperpot came by, carrying both the sheaf of corn and the little bird-house.

The young lady gave him a dazzling smile and said: 'Oh, Mr Pepperpot, wouldn't you like to buy a wreath of mistletoe for your wife?'

'No thanks,' said Mr Pepperpot, 'I'm in a hurry.'

'Swing high! Swing low! I'm in the mistletoe!' sang Mrs Pepperpot from her lofty perch.

When Mr Pepperpot caught sight of her his mouth fell open: 'Oh dear!' he groaned, 'this is too bad!'

With a shaking hand he paid the young lady the right money and lifted the wreath down himself, taking care that Mrs Pepperpot didn't slip out of his fingers. This time there would be no escape; he would take his wife straight home, whether she liked it or not. But just as he was leaving, the young lady said: 'Oh, Sir, you're our one hundredth customer, so you get a free balloon!' and she handed him a red balloon.

Before anyone could say 'Jack Robinson' Mrs Pepperpot had grabbed the string and, while Mr Pepperpot was struggling with his purse, gloves and parcels, his tiny wife was soaring up into the sky. Up she went over the market-place, and soon she was fluttering over the trees of the forest, followed by a crowd of crows and magpies and small birds of every sort.

'Here I come!' she shouted in bird-language. For, when Mrs Pepperpot was small she could talk with animals and birds.

A big crow cawed: 'Are you going to the moon with that balloon?'

'Not quite, I hope!' said Mrs Pepperpot, and she told them the whole story. The birds all squawked with glee when they heard about the corn and the birdhouse she had got for them.

'But first you must help me,' said Mrs Pepperpot. 'I want you all to hang on to this balloon string and guide me back to land on my own doorstep.'

So the birds clung to the string with their beaks and claws and, as they flew down to Mrs Pepperpot's house, the balloon looked like a kite with fancy bows tied to its tail.

When Mrs Pepperpot set foot on the ground she instantly grew to her normal size.

So she waved good-bye to the birds and went indoors to wait for Mr Pepperpot.

It was late in the evening before Mr Pepperpot came home, tired and miserable after searching everywhere for his lost wife. He put his knapsack down in the hall and carried the sheaf of corn and the bird-house outside. But when he came in again he noticed that the mistletoe had disappeared.

'Oh well,' he said sadly, 'what does it matter now that Mrs Pepperpot is gone?'

He opened the door into the kitchen; there was the mistletoe hanging over the doorway and, under it, as large as life, stood Mrs Pepperpot!

'Darling husband!' she said, as she put her arms round his neck and gave him a great big smacking kiss:

'Happy Christmas!'